T☢XIC

❝ He turned quickly to his right, but all he saw was the sea gently rolling up onto the beach.

But when he turned to his left, his heart froze.

Snaking its way out of the jungle next to the sea, and whacking its tail on the ground, was a large, scaly, terrifying looking crocodile. **❞**

ISLAND SHOCK

Island Shock
by Jonny Zucker
Illustrated by Kerry Ingham

Published by Ransom Publishing Ltd.
Unit 7, Brocklands Farm, West Meon, Hampshire
GU32 1JN, UK
www.ransom.co.uk

ISBN   978 178127 711 9
First published in 2015
Reprinted 2015

ISLAND SHOCK

JONNY ZUCKER

ILLUSTRATED BY
KERRY INGHAM

Ransom

CHAPTER 1

Mike Chen woke up with a start.

He opened his eyes slowly and had to hold up his hand to protect them from a glaring light.

The last thing he remembered was falling asleep at the airport terminal, where he'd been waiting to catch a plane.

He lowered his hand and was astonished by the sight that greeted him.

He was on a beach.

Sand stretched all around him. Gentle waters from a vast ocean lapped onto the shore. A couple of huge trees bearing strange orange fruit stood a short distance away on the sand.

There was no sign of Mac or Robbie, or any of the other kids from school who'd been waiting with him for the plane to France.

What on Earth was going on? Where was he – and how had he got here?

He scanned the ground for his rucksack. He couldn't see it.

Maybe Mr Masters had tricked them all, and instead of going to France he'd taken them to some remote island.

But if that was true, where were the others?

'MAC! ROBBIE! MR MASTERS!' he called.

Nothing. Just the sound of the sea.

Scratching his head in total bewilderment, Mike stood up and looked behind him.

A jungle of trees, bushes and wild grass lay before him, stretching into the distance as far as he could see.

It looked like he was on an island – one of those desert islands you sometimes see in the movies.

But it was impossible to tell from here how big the island was. It might be no more than a hundred metres. It might be thirty times that size.

Mike realised he was incredibly thirsty. He walked towards the trees and saw a small rock pool, fed by a tiny stream.

Crouching down, he cupped his hands and dipped them into the pool. Drinking from his hands, he was pleased to find that the water wasn't salty.

At least he had fresh water.

He had just splashed some water on his face when he heard a thumping sound a short way away.

He turned quickly to his right, but all he saw was the sea gently rolling up onto the beach.

When he turned to his left however, his heart froze.

Snaking its way out of the jungle next to the sea, and whacking its tail on the ground, was a large, scaly, terrifying-looking crocodile.

CHAPTER 2

A CROCODILE!

The crocodile locked eyes with Mike and slithered rapidly in his direction, its huge body making deep imprints in the sand.

Mike looked around.

This couldn't be happening! A crocodile was only a few metres away – and it didn't look friendly.

Where should he go? What could he do?

He had to get away from the crocodile, but what would happen if he fell into a ditch or tripped over some rocks?

What if it outran him? The green killer would be on him.

Defending yourself from a crocodile attack wasn't something they taught you at school.

The croc was starting to move faster, its body twisting and turning as it sped across the sand. Its fiery eyes gave the impression that it could do with a good meal.

Mike started sprinting for the nearest of the two fruit trees. He wasn't a brilliant climber, but he'd had a couple of goes on the climbing wall at his local leisure centre.

He hared across the sand, the crocodile racing after him, snapping at his heels.

It nearly caught the back of his shoe in its mouth, but Mike kicked it off and sped up.

It was almost on him again when he launched himself through the air. Catching onto the lower branches of the first tree, he pulled himself up.

The branch wasn't very strong, so he found a foothold and climbed up to a thicker one.

The crocodile waited at the bottom of the tree, opening and closing its mouth and making a horrible roaring sound.

Mike pulled at one of the orange fruits and chucked it down. It missed the croc by a very short distance.

The second one hit it on the top of its head. It wheeled round in anger.

He threw a third and a fourth one, both of them whacking the crocodile.

Swishing its tail furiously, the crocodile admitted defeat and slowly slunk away.

A couple of minutes later it had disappeared back into the jungle.

His body still shaking with fear, Mike waited another twenty minutes before he carefully climbed down.

CHAPTER 3

The sun was still burning hot, but Mike could see that the end of the day was not too far off.

His instinct was to go and search the rest of the island straight away.

There might be other people who could tell him how he got here and how he would be able to get away.

There might even be some sort of hotel or guesthouse.

But if he went on too long a search and found nothing, he would have wasted vital time. And with no obvious means of escape, he needed to do something quickly.

First, he gathered a large collection of branches and sticks that he could use as weapons if the crocodile – or any other fierce creature – attacked.

Then he searched the shoreline and the grass and got together a big pile of rocks, pieces of wood and large leaves.

Making stuff was one of his favourite things to do, and within a couple of hours he'd built himself a basic shack, raised above the round on stilts and with enough room for him to lie down.

He placed lengths of wood and large leaves from some of the jungle trees on top to give his shelter a solid roof. A few large leaves served as his front door.

Hopefully his new home would keep the crocodile – and any other creatures – at bay.

*****

It was starting to get dark. Hunger began nudging his insides.

Mike grabbed one of the fruits he'd thrown at the crocodile and, using a pointed stick, dug out some of the orange flesh.

He tried a little bit of it on his tongue. Thankfully it was tasty.

Hungrily, Mike ate all of the fruit and cut open a few more. He hoped they weren't poisonous.

He drank another few handfuls of water from the rock pool and put the finishing touches to the shack.

Then he looked up and watched the last flecks of the day's sun disappear below the horizon, before darkness cloaked the island.

Getting into the shack, he moved his body around until he was as comfortable as he could get. He placed his stick-and-branch weapons beside him.

Some kind of animal made a distant wailing sound.

At least, Mike *thought* it was an animal.

It took him a while to get to sleep, and when he finally did drift off his dreams were filled with large, green, angry crocodiles.

CHAPTER 4

It was a slimy brown cockroach that woke Mike. It was crawling over his arm.

Even though cockroaches back home didn't bother him, this one was far larger than any he'd seen before. It was easily as large as his hand.

'EUURGHH, DISGUSTING!' he shouted, throwing his arm to one side and sending the cockroach flying.

But there was another one on his leg, and a third on his other arm.

'GET OFF!' he yelled, frantically brushing them off, kicking open the shack's front door and pushing himself outside.

Another cockroach was on his chest and a fifth was on his knee.

There were two more on the top of his head …

Now there was one on his cheek …

They were awful, and they smelt pretty bad too.

Screaming, Mike grabbed a branch from the shack and started whacking them all off.

They flew off him and hit the ground, before scuttling away in all directions and disappearing.

Mike vowed to himself that he'd close every gap in the walls and roof of his home before he went to sleep that night.

No more cockroach wake-up calls.

After drinking some water and eating some fruit, Mike made some improvements to his shack. Making the walls stronger and less porous took a long time.

He sat under the shade of a fruit tree while the sun was at its hottest, and it was mid-afternoon before he started off, walking along the shore and keeping an eye out for any crocodiles.

*****

Mike hadn't got very far when he came up against an old rusty fence which ran down the beach and into the sea. A sign was stuck to it.

KEEP OUT!
DANGER OF DEATH!

So people *did* live on the island. Or at least, they had once lived here.

Mike was tempted to scale the fence and explore further, but the prospect of death wasn't a very inviting one.

He sighed with frustration and turned back.

He had only gone a few metres when he heard a rasping noise above him. He looked up just in time to see a large black cloud and a circle of raindrops falling towards him.

But this wasn't normal rain. It was hail, and these were large silver hailstones, as big as table-tennis balls.

One hit him on the cheek and it felt like he'd just been whacked with a rock.

Mike started running back along the beach, but the hailstones continued, as if they were following him, smashing down on him wherever he went.

He put his hands over his head to protect himself and sped up.

These were killer hailstones. He had to escape them.

But as he ran Mike twisted his foot on a stray branch and he fell onto his back.

He lay there, staring up in horror at the flying silver bullets that continued to rain down on him.

CHAPTER 5

Knowing he had to find shelter from the hailstones or risk getting seriously injured, Mike rolled over to his right and took refuge under a fruit tree.

The hail continued falling, but the tree provided shelter and Mike was spared any more attacks.

Panting and sweating, he waited until the hailstorm started moving away, and after turning a corner of the island it was out of sight.

Mike stroked his cheek and slumped down onto the ground.

Was this all a dream – a hideous nightmare?

If it was, it was the longest and most gruesome one he'd ever had. In less than twenty-four hours he'd been attacked by a crocodile, invaded by giant slimy cockroaches and rained on by rock-hard hailstones.

And where had the violent hailstorm come from? The sky was now a deep shade of royal blue and completely cloudless, just as it had been before the sudden hailstorm.

It didn't make any sense.

Slowly, he walked back along the beach to his shack, questions continuing to flow freely.

Could he have mistakenly taken the wrong plane while Mr Masters and his mates had taken the correct one to France?

But if that was the case, how had he ended up alone on this island? How would he have got here after getting off the plane? Surely someone from the flight crew or the airport would have woken him up before he got here?

He ate some more fruit and tried to gather his thoughts.

Still with no answers, he decided that his next step would be a trek into the heart of the island. There might be a settlement, or at least a few houses, away from the shoreline.

Just as Mike turned to start his trek inland, a large yellow bush suddenly lurched towards him and a tough brown stem wrapped itself around his waist.

'GET OFF ME!' he shouted, but the stem tightened its grip, digging into his body.

Chapter 6

This couldn't be happening!

In shock and horror, Mike grabbed the stem and started uncurling it, but it pulled him towards the bush and resisted his efforts.

This was monstrous: a death-seeking bush was attacking him.

He went at the stem again and, with a huge effort, managed to prise himself free.

But while he was doing this, another tendril shot out from the bush and spread itself around his chest, while another made for his feet.

With panic rising inside him, Mike kicked at the tendril attacking his foot and it fell away, but the stem wrapped around his chest was squeezing him harder and harder.

Snatching at the stem with both hands, he pulled at it with every ounce of strength and threw it off, allowing him to breathe properly again.

He leapt backwards as another of the evil tendrils tried to encircle his head.

He was free!

As quickly as he could manage, he turned and ran. As he ran, he looked back over his shoulder and saw the tendrils slowly retreating back into the bush, like wounded soldiers.

However shaken and shocked Mike was at that moment, he gritted his teeth and started striding away from the shore, further into the jungle, towards the centre of the island.

That had been his plan and he was sticking to it.

*****

He'd been walking for well over an hour when a large rusty fence blocked his path. It stretched before him, to the left and right, as far as he could see.

The fence bore a sign.

KEEP OUT!
DANGER OF DEATH!

It was exactly like the other sign on the beach.

Mike retraced his steps and set off on another path through the jungle.

The trees here were very densely packed and their brown branches and light green leaves formed a canopy above his head.

He heard twigs snapping on either side of him, presumably as a result of being stepped on by small jungle animals.

He wiped the sweat off his face and told himself off for not bringing any water with him.

But time was of the essence and he was aware it would be getting dark soon. He

wasn't in the mood for turning back. He needed to keep going.

Mike weaved past several bushes – identical to the ones that had pounced on him – and steered around a line of odd-looking trees.

Up ahead he spotted the start of a twisting mud trail and his spirits lifted. Maybe this path led somewhere useful.

Maybe his ordeal was nearly at an end.

But as he made for the start of the path, he heard a loud rustle in the bushes and a huge grey dog, fiercer and larger than a wolf, leaped through the air towards him, its fangs sparkling in the sunlight.

CHAPTER 7

Mike dived to his left and the dog went crashing past him, growling wildly, gnashing its teeth and spinning around to face him again.

In an instant, Mike picked up a large branch from the jungle floor. Shouting at the top of his voice, he thrust the branch at the dog.

Snarling with rage, it tried to wrestle the branch from him with its fierce jaws. Huge drops of saliva cascaded out of its mouth.

For a few seconds they struggled, the branch in between them, the dog's barks and growls getting louder and more menacing by the second.

But with a ferocious tug Mike pulled the branch away from the dog's grasp and raised it in the air. He then brought it crashing down.

As the shadow of the branch loomed over the dog, it yelped in fear, spun round and went sprinting off into the trees.

A moment later it was gone.

Mike fell to his knees and dropped the branch.

This was getting unbearable. Whichever direction he took, grave danger was lurking, waiting for his approach.

With the branch still in his hand, he got to his feet, listened for any further noises from the dog and stepped onto the twisting path.

He checked all around him every few seconds, in case something else wanted to attack him, but he walked for half an hour without incident.

*****

The sun was setting when he jumped over a large nest of green ants, turned a corner and was halted in his tracks.

A sandy path began in a few metres, but in front of it stretched a large rusty wire fence. Nailed to it was another sign.

KEEP OUT!
DANGER OF DEATH!

In frustration and anger Mike hit a nearby tree with the palm of his hand. It was impossible to get anywhere.

It was time for him to face facts.

He was stranded, without any provisions, except for a rock pool of water and some strange orange fruit.

No one was here. He was totally alone.

He was never going to get off the island.

CHAPTER 8

Mike stared angrily at the sign. Having his way blocked for a third time was beyond frustrating.

But then a thought suddenly struck him. Hadn't he already faced terrible dangers?

The crocodile, the cockroaches, the hailstones, the bush stems and now the wolf dog. What could be worse than those?

And anyway, maybe the danger signs had been put up years and years ago, when there *was* some kind of danger.

What if that danger no longer existed? What if the signs were out of date?

Mike chewed his bottom lip thinking about this. He didn't fancy dying, but perhaps the only way of finding out why he was here was to get over that fence.

However, it was getting really dark now. Shouldn't he go back while there was still enough light to guide him?

A feeling of strength welled up in his chest.

No. He would go on.

He began climbing the fence. It was the work of less than thirty seconds to scale it and jump down on the other side.

On he went, walking down the sandy path, moving his eyes rapidly from right to left, looking out for any hint of danger in the disappearing light. If he saw anything really bad he would turn back and clamber over the fence.

The path led to a large wood of skinny, brown trees. On the other side was a wide stone track.

Mike listened out for signs of danger, but all he could hear was the night breeze.

Continuing on the track for another ten minutes, he saw a large formation of rock in the distance. As he approached the rock he

saw a thin strip of light shining out from inside it.

Mike frowned.

Silently, he stepped right up to the rock and placed his eye against the crack through which the light was shining.

His heart jolted in shock.

It was a cave.

And inside the cave was a group of humans.

CHAPTER 9

Mike was too stunned to move for a few moments.

Who was in there? Were they island tribes-people? And if they were, what would they do to him if they found him?

Terrified and excited at the same time, he found some footholds and handholds and started climbing up the side of the rock. At the top he found a much larger crack.

He peered through.

Inside the cave were lots of TV screens, crates of equipment he didn't recognise, cables and sound microphones.

Sitting round a table were six people; three women and three men.

They didn't look like tribes-people. They were all wearing shorts, T-shirts and sandals.

'Shall we put Mike's fight with the dog at the start of tonight's programme, Tony?' asked one of the women.

She reached into a dark corner and pulled out a large wild dog, just like the one that had attacked Mike.

She flicked a button on a black panel and the dog started moving its head and growling. She flicked another button and it stopped.

Mike stared down in shock.

The wild dog that had attacked him wasn't real! It was some kind of robot.

Then another woman switched on a TV screen and Mike watched, with those below him, the fight he'd had with the dog.

She paused it as Mike waved the stick and the dog bolted.

Tony – who seemed to be in charge – grinned.

'Yes, it's always good to get some fight action at the start. I'll go down to the boat in a bit and call the studio on the satellite phone. They'll love the dog battle! Mike really went for that hound!'

The others laughed.

Mike felt an icy stab rip through him.

He looked round the cave and spotted, tucked away at the back, parts of a mechanical crocodile, some robotic cockroaches, a large crate of the huge hailstones and a model of the bush with the stems.

None of them were real. They were all electronic gizmos.

With a horrible twinge of anger in his chest, Mike now realised what was going on.

This group of people had somehow got him to the island without him knowing.

And now they were making a TV series about him!

They'd put all of those dangers in his way just to see how he would react to them.

And the DANGER signs? They'd put them up to keep him from finding out the truth.

The whole thing was a set up!

Fury rose inside Mike.

He saw a temporary light switch rigged on the wall near the entrance to the cave and a torch on the floor, just below it.

Clambering back down, he crept to the entrance and poked his hand inside the cave.

Then all at once he grabbed the torch from the floor and turned off the lights, while making a series of terrifying, blood-curdling roars.

CHAPTER 10

The film crew instantly panicked.

They screamed and ran in all directions, knocking the table over and sending coffee cups smashing onto the ground.

'What's going on?' shouted someone.

'Get the lights on!' yelled someone else.

But however hard they tried, they couldn't find the light switch.

Mike flicked on the torch and raced away. Climbing back over the fence, he hurtled back to his shack.

*****

As soon as he arrived back at his shack, Mike started running round the edge of the water, circling the island in the same direction he'd gone earlier.

When he came to the DANGER sign he'd seen previously, he climbed over it and kept going.

It took him fifteen minutes to reach the far side of the island. When he arrived he smiled with delight.

For there, with water lapping against its side, was a large boat.

He could hear the film crew in the distance, shouting and bawling and crashing though the trees.

Mike stepped onto the boat's lower deck. He passed mounds of equipment – cameras, lights, electrical cables and sound microphones.

And in an open case was the satellite phone he'd heard them talking about in the cave.

He heard cries coming from the jungle, but he ignored them.

He moved his torch over the inside of the boat and saw comfy bedrooms with beds, proper showers and toilets.

This was obviously where the film crew slept – while he'd been roughing it out on the beach!

Climbing up a short flight of stairs, he reached the bridge with plenty of electronic gadgets, a steering wheel and an ignition button.

A smile played on his face.

'WHO IS THAT?' shouted a voice from the shore.

It was the voice of Tony, the director.

In an instant Mike pushed the ignition button and the boat's engine roared into life.

'HEY!' yelled Tony, running along the sand. 'YOU CAN'T DO THAT!'

But the boat was already pulling away from the shore, with Mike gripping the steering wheel and checking out all of the other buttons.

'Please!' screamed Tony. 'You've got our satellite phone. It's the only way we can contact the mainland!'

'So you'll have a longer stay!' shouted Mike back. 'Maybe you could make a TV show about it!'

Tony fell to his knees on the sand, wailing like a baby and waving his fists.

'NOOOOO!' he shrieked.

But Mike didn't look back.

It wasn't long before the rear lights of the boat had disappeared into the night, carrying its one very relieved and delighted crew-member.

Now read the first chapter of another great
Toxic title by Jonny Zucker:

GLADIATOR
REVIVAL

CHAPTER 1

THWACK!

A metal-tipped spear shot down the tunnel a centimetre above Nick and Kat's head.

'WHAT'S GOING ON?' shouted Kat in panic.

'I DON'T KNOW!' replied Nick. 'BUT RUN!'

*****

Ten minutes ago, Nick and Kat Ellis had been staring up at Rome's giant Coliseum. They were on holiday and they'd split from their parents for a few hours.

Nick had spotted a tattered door on the other side of the road and he'd insisted they open it and explore.

He was a boy who loved adventure.

The door had led to this dimly lit, downward-sloping tunnel.

They'd only gone a few paces when the spear had been launched at them.

*****

THWACK!

There was another one, bouncing off the tunnel wall with a horrible clanging echo.

In horror, they upped their speed, terrified of being hit.

'LOOK! UP AHEAD!' shouted Nick.

They could see a circle of light at the end of the tunnel. Sprinting towards it, they ran into what looked exactly like an ancient Roman market.

People in old Roman clothes were selling fruit, vegetables and coloured spices. Strange gold coins were being passed between customers and stallholders.

'THIS WAY!' barked Nick, leaping out of the way of another flying spear.

They raced between some squawking chickens and leapt over a pile of logs.

They'd just run through an archway at the far end of the market when they were suddenly surrounded.

Four huge men in silver-coloured, ancient Roman armour – helmets, tunics and iron breastplates – were looming over them, spears raised in the air.

'I guess your little journey has just ended,' said one of the soldiers.

He and the other soldiers raised their spears to strike.

MORE GREAT TOXIC READS

Action-packed adventure stories featuring jungles, swamps, deserted islands, robots, space travel, zombies, computer viruses and monsters from the deep.

How many have you read?

THE BATTLE OF THE UNDERSEA KINGDOM

by Jonny Zucker

When the local mayor is kidnapped, the people suspect other villages of taking him. But Danny's dad, Tyler, knows more. He thinks that creatures from under the sea are to blame – and he's going to prove it!

MORE GREAT TOXIC READS

FOOTBALL FORCE

by Jonny Zucker

It's 2066 and football has changed. Players now wear lightweight body armour. Logan Smith wants to play for the best local team – Vestige United. Their players are fantastic, but Logan suspects that the team has a dark secret.

GLADIATOR REVIVAL

by Jonny Zucker

Nick and Kat are on holiday in Rome with their parents. So how do they end up facing the perils of the Coliseum in ancient Rome – as gladiators? Is somebody making a film? Or is this for real and they are fighting for their lives?

MORE GREAT TOXIC READS

CRASH LAND EARTH

by Jonny Zucker

Jed and his friends are setting out on a trip to Mars. But their spaceship is in trouble and they are forced to crash-land back on Earth. But nothing is quite as it should be. Jed and his fellow explorers find themselves in a race against time to save planet Earth.

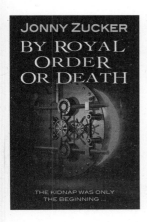

BY ROYAL ORDER OR DEATH

by Jonny Zucker

Miles is a member of the Royal Protection Hub, whose job is to protect the Royal family. When Princess Helena is kidnapped, Miles uncovers a cunning and dangerous plot. Miles must use all his skills to outwit the kidnappers and save the princess's life.

Jonny Zucker has been a teacher, musician, stand-up comedian and footballer, but now he is best known as one of the most popular authors for children. So far he has written over 100 books.

Jonny also plays in a band and has done over 60 gigs as a stand-up comedian, reaching the London Region Final of the BBC New Comedy awards.

He still dreams of being a professional footballer.